고양이들은 어디로 갔을까?

Where have all the cats gone?

박자현
Park Jahyun

In 2014, spring, I found a neighboring village had shattered.
Even though I have lived nearby,
I have not noticed that the village had been disappearing.
Since then, I have been looking for such disappearing areas,
so-called designated 'redevelopment area'.
There, I could encounter stray cats between rubble in the ruined villages.
That spring, I witnessed houses destined to be demolished,
and cats lying down on the roof of collapsed houses got injured and withered.
The cats I met and draw were found at Motgol, Daeyoen 4-dong,
Manduck Daechunamoo(meaning jujube tree), Jangjeong 3dong.
The areas are being destroyed, or people say, 'redevelopment' is in the making now.
Whenever I saw the debris,
I wonder where all the cats which had dwell there have gone now.
May peace be with the cats.

2014년 봄, 옆 마을이 전쟁터처럼 부서진 것을 보게 되었다. 가까이 있었지만 이웃 마을이 사라지는 소리를 듣지 못했다. 그 이후로 계속해서 부산에 재개발 지역을 찾아다녔다. 부서져가는 그곳에 살고 있는 고양이들을 보게 되었다. 곧 사라질 마을들, 지붕 위에 누워 햇볕을 받으며 옹기종기 모여 있던 봄 이후 고양이들은 크게 상처입고 말라갔다.

그려진 고양이들은 부산의 못골, 대연 4동, 만덕 대추나무골, 장전 3동의 고양이들이다. 이곳 마을들은 이미 사라졌거나 사라지는 중이고 대연롯데캐슬레전드, 대연파크프루지오, LH, 래미안이 지어지는 중이다. 부서진 집터를 볼 때 마다 이곳에 살던 고양이들은 어디로 갔을까 궁금해진다. 부디 잘 이사했기를..

주소 잃은

address that they lost

내가 그를 바라보고, 사진을 찍고, 그림을 그려도
그에 대해 적을 수 있는 사실은
그가 결국은 떠나야 하는 다 부서져 내리는 그의 동네 이름.

2015년 1월. 부산 대연 4동에서 만난 고양이. 가려진 천 안에서

I look in them, take photo of them, and draw them.
But the only information I could tell about them was the names of villages
where they would leave soon in the end.

Jannuary, 2015. Daneyoen 4dong, Busan. A cat covered by a cloth.

6

한때는 누군가에게 먹는 물로, 몸을 씻는 물로, 삶을 살 수 있게 했던 물이 담겨있던
버려진 푸른색 물탱크 앞에서 인형처럼 가만히 앉아.

2015년 1월. 부산 대연 4동.

A cat sitting still, being looked like statue before a blue cistern.
This blue cistern would contain life-saving water before being abandoned like this.

January, 2015. Daeyoen 4dong, Busan.

 ,,,,8

오전 11시경 역광을 받으며 강아지풀이 만발한 언덕을 오르던 고양이가
빈 그릇을 들여다보다가 나를 쳐다본다.
말라있는 강아지풀도 갈색, 고양이도 갈색.

2015년 1월. 부산 대연 4동.

11 Am, a cat is staring at me. The cat is walking up the sunlit hill full of bristle grass.
Brownish bristle grass, bristle cat.

January, 2015. Daeyoen 4dong, Busan.

너는 앞으로 어디로 이사 가니? 롯데캐슬레전드가 들어설 자리.
대부분의 집들이 사라져 황무지로 변하고 자동차 그늘 아래서 나를 경계하고 앉은 고양이.

2015년 2월. 대연 6동.

Where will be your next shelter? The area is designated as an area for developing
apartment buildings being named Lottle Castle.
Most houses existed before have been removed and now here has turned to a wide wasteland.
A cat was staring at me under the shadows of car.

February, 2015. Daeyoen6 dong, Busan.

"동네가 사라지면 고양이들은 다른 동네로 이사 가겠지?"

"그렇겠지"

"철거되고 동네가 없어지는 과정에서 다치는 고양이들도 있겠지?"

다른 마을로 가서 새로운 터를 잡는 데 많이 힘들 것 같아."

폐허에 누가 뼈다귀를 두고 갔을까?

그 뼈다귀를 지키며 나를 보고 바짝 긴장한 고양이.

2015년 2월. 대연 6동.

"People who have lived here will move, and houses are disappearing,
and the cats also have to move to somewhere?
"Probably so"
"In the process of demolition, some cats got injured?
It would be tough for the cats to find a new shelter for them.
Who left a bone at this deserted land?
A cat is holding tightly, and is seeing me watchfully.

February, 2015. Daeyoen6 dong, Busan.

무너진 집터 버려진 넝마 위에 몸을 누이고 나에게 적의조차 보일 힘없이 가늘게 뜬 두 눈.
그림 속 고양이의 두 눈이 그때의 나와 지금의 나를 부끄럽게 만든다.
2017년 9월 이곳에 래미안이 들어온다.
이곳 래미안의 분양권이 200:1이었다고.
그 이후 재개발이라는 무너뜨림이 더 무섭게 힘을 얻었던 것 같다.

2015년 초 겨울 폐허가 되어가는 부산 장전 3지구를 지나다 보게 된 고양이.

The cat looked too helpless to be alert of this invader. Her eyes were almost closed.
The cat's eyes in the photo feel like have 'me then' overlap 'me now'.
In 2017, September, famous brand name apartment Raemian will replace here as new housing buildings.
A source said the competition rate to get housing distribution was as much as 200:1. Since then,
'destructions' under the mask of 'redevelopment' has started to gather momentum.

2015, early winter. I walked through Jangjeong 3dong, Busan.
I saw a cat lying on ragged clothes among crumbled houses.

깊고 어두운 덤불 속에 숨어있는 친구를 지키며 햇볕 속에 앉아 있는 고양이.
침입자에게 이내 경계를 풀고 편안한 눈길로 나를 바라보았던.
지금은 이 길이 모두 사라져버렸다.
황새알 마을을 모두 무너뜨리고 그 옆 마을에 황새알 우물터 복원 공사를 하고
황새알 마을의 역사적 가치를 새롭게 발굴한다는 일주일 전 뉴스.
마을과 그 많던 우물터들은 이제 없다.

2015년 6월. 부산 황새알 마을.

On the road, I encountered a cat in the sun.
She looked like guarding other cats hiding in the dark thicket.
But she soon let down her guard against this invader (me), and saw me with gentle eyes.
These roads in this village have disappeared.
News a week ago said, Hwangsaeal village would be flattened to the grand
and reconstruction of old well is expected.
However, now I cannot find any well in this village.

June, 2015. Hwangsaeal village, Busan.

아무것도 들고 있지 않던 나를 한참이나 바라보며 그릇 앞에 앉아 있었다.
그때부터 매주 황새알 마을을 찾아가 고양이들을 만났는데
마을은 대부분 무너지고 내 마음도 빠르게 무심해져 갔다.

2015년 6월. 부산 황새알 마을.

Since, almost every week, I visit this ruined village (Hwangsaeal Maeul), and met stray cats.
The village was collapsing more rapidly, and I could feel my heart was getting numb rapidly too.

June, 2015. Hwangaeal village, Busan.

빠르게 무너뜨려 졌던 황새알 마을의 10월, 나는 집에서 그곳의 고양이를 그린다.
작은 방들과 바닥에 버려진 오래된 그릇들. 뜨거운 햇볕,
남아있던 대추나무 그늘아래 나를 만나 누워 쉬던 고양이.
누워있는 몸 위로 덮힌 햇살. 한참을 서로의 눈을 쳐다보았다.

2015년 7월. 부산 황새알 마을.

In October that year, I was drawing the cats I found in Hwangsaeal village.
I recalled the cats taking rest under jujube tree, sunshine, abandoned glass plates.
Sunshine spotlights the cat's body. The cat and I was seeing each other quite long.

July, 2015. Hawngaeal village, Busan.

고양이들이 모여 사는 못골 언덕에 한 채 남은 집.
언젠가 이 집도 부서질 것이고 롯데캐슬 레전드가 들어온다.
며칠 전 누군가가 요즘은 부모님들이 집에 못 찾아오게끔 아파트 이름을 영어로 짓는다고 했다.
이 한 채 남은 집에 상처 입고 아픈 고양이들이 모여 산다.
몸에 상처가 보이지 않고 아마도 그래서 우리를 반겨줄 수 있었던 고양이.

2015년 10월. 부산 대연 6동.

On Motgol hill, only one house was left, where many cats have lived together.
In this last house, injured, hurt cats are continuing their life.
Someday, this house will be torn down soon.
Lotte Castle Legend will be built here.
A cat which looks comparatively healthy seemed to greet me.

November, 2015. Daeyeong 6dong, Busan.

못골 입구에 한 채 있던, 고양이들이 모여 살던 집은 사라졌다.

롯데캐슬레전드는 지어지는데 고양이들은 다들 어디로 쫓겨났을까?

"여기에 들어설 아파트가 얼마고 얼마나 오를 거고 하는 이야기는 많이 하지만

마을이 철거 돼서 원치 않게 흩어진 사람들이 어디에서 어떻게 살고 있는지 아무도 궁금해하지 않아요."

"의지가 사라지고 있어요. 하지만 뭐라도 해야 하지 않겠어요?

이대로 떠날 수 없으니까. 뭐라도 하지 않을 수 없으니까."

······ 만덕주민공동체

The last house in Motgol village has eventually gone.

The apartment complex Lotte Castle Legend started to be built.

Now where all the cats that dwelled here have disappeared?

"People are talking about enthusiastically at which price the apartment would be trade,

and how much profit they make if their trade is successful.

But now one is interested in those people who have lived here but had to leave by force.

"The will to fight is diminishing, but we have to do something, right."

We should not leave here doing nothing. We should do something.

······ Speak out from Manduck Daechoonanmoo Gol community.

못골 고양이들이 함께 사는 집. 2018년 2월 롯데캐슬이 세워질 것이다.
고양이가 모여 사는 집에서 보았던 가장 아픈 고양이.
잠자는 것처럼 보이던 고양이가 천천히 고개를 돌리자 나의 숨이 더 더뎌졌다.
캐슬, 레전드 이런 이름들을 왜 거주지 이름에 붙이는 걸까?
이제 그곳의 비둘기길, 동암동 산길, 흥암길들은 모두 지워지고 거대한 사막 언덕이 되었다.

2015년 10월에 만났던 고양이.

The house where cat have dwell in crowds. Apparently, the cat looked lethargic.
She looked like almost sleeping. When the cat turned her head to me,
I felt my heart pound slower, but now relieved.
Castle, Legend, such English words,
how can these English words be used for calling apartments buildings?
It's bizzare to use such English words when you write an address.
This areas were called 'Bidoolgi Gil'(meaning Dove Road),
Doamdongsan gil, Heungam Gil.
Those names were erased and now they look like a wide desert in a city.

A cat I met on October 2015.

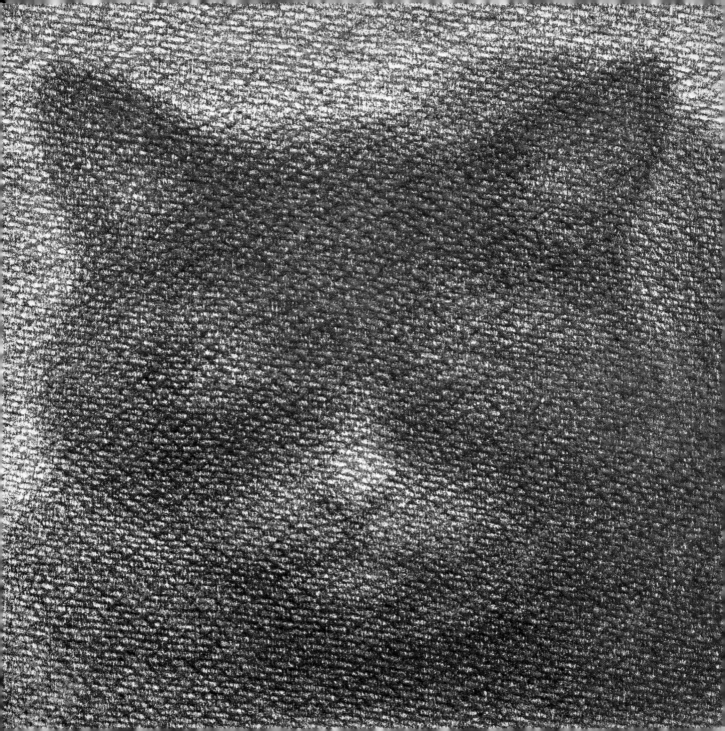

못골에는 집이 몇 채 남지 않았다. 그곳에 고양이들이 모여 산다.
자기 영역을 중시하는 고양이가 그 동네를 떠나지 못하고 함께 살기로,
함께 살아 간다는 것이, 그 집은 두드릴 문이 없다.

2015년 10월. 부산 못골.

Only few houses have been left in Motgol village.
Cats still remained in Motgol is still continuing their life.
As far as I know, cats are very private creatures, but they are living together in huddle,
in a house without any door to protect them from invader.

October, 2015. Motgol village, Busan.

"처음엔 울분이었어요. 어떻게 해야 할지도 몰랐어요.
억울하고 화가 나니까 거리로 나갔지요. 우리는 알아야만했어요.
우리에게 일어난 일이 무엇인지, 삶이 나아지는 일이라고 하는데, 왜 우리를 밀어내는 건지."
"우리는 오래도록 싸웠어요. 과정에서 이겼지만, 결과는 졌어요.
'어쩔 수 있나' 그게 우리가 들은 마지막 말이었어요."
······ 만덕주민공동체

2019년 명륜자이가 들어설 마을에 고양이.

"At first, we had anger and did not figure out how to deal with it.
We thought it's not right, and it's definitely unlawful, so we had to take it to street.
And we wanted to know what's happening.
They told us life would be better, but why they kick out us from where we have lived?"
"We have fought quite long. We were winner in process, but we were defeated.
'What else can we do?' I'm afraid there's nothing we can. That's what we said lastly."
······ Speak out from Manduck Daechoonanmoo Gol community.

Cat in the place designated to build Zai Apartment, Myungryoon dong.

"부산시에서만 재개발이 진행 중인 마을이 194개에요."

"부산시에서만 사라지는 마을이 194개에요."

"겁이나요. 이웃집이 비어져가고 앞집이 무너지는 소리에 잠이 깨고,

무너진 집들이 길에 널려 있고, 그 집들을 밟고 지나다녀야 하는 게 무섭고 슬퍼요.

하지만 우리는 우리들 집에 있어요. 그래야 지킬 수 있어요."

······ 만덕주민공동체

2016년 3월. 명륜동. 흐려지고 지워지는 얼굴, 마을.

"In Busan, as many as 194 villages are designated for redevelopment areas.

In other words as many as 194 old villages are disappearing."

"It's terrifying. In my neighboring houses, there's no one living.

And we often wake up by the sound of noise generated when tearing down houses.

Here are piles of rubble left in the wake of demolition of houses.

We were scared and frustrated with the reality we have to walk on the debris.

But we are still staying in our houses. We won't leave to keep our houses."

······ Speak out from Manduck Daechoonanmoo Gol community.

March, 2016, Myungryoon dong. A face blurred and erased.

슬레이트 지붕 위에서 눈을 떴다 감았다.
지치고 힘없는 모습에 3년 전 할머니들 초상화 그리는 일을 할 때가 생각났다.
몸이 약하시고 오르막을 걷기 힘든 할머니들은
이곳처럼 가파른 언덕을 올라야만 만날 수 있는 곳에 살고계셨다.
평지에는 비교적 젊은 사람들이 살아간다.
평지에 있는 마을이 재개발되면 할머니들과 함께 고양이들도 높은 곳으로 쫓겨나겠지?

2016년 4월. 서동언덕 마을의 맨 위쪽까지 올라가서 보게 된 고양이.

The cat open eyes and close eyes again and again.
Her helpless and feeble appearance remind me of the time when I drew senior persons.
The senior persons also mostly live in uphill villages. Younger people tend to live in downtowns.
When redevelopment construction of old downtown areas is completed,
would older persons and stray cats be expelled to tacky uphill villages?

April, 2016. A cat on the top of the hill Seodong village.

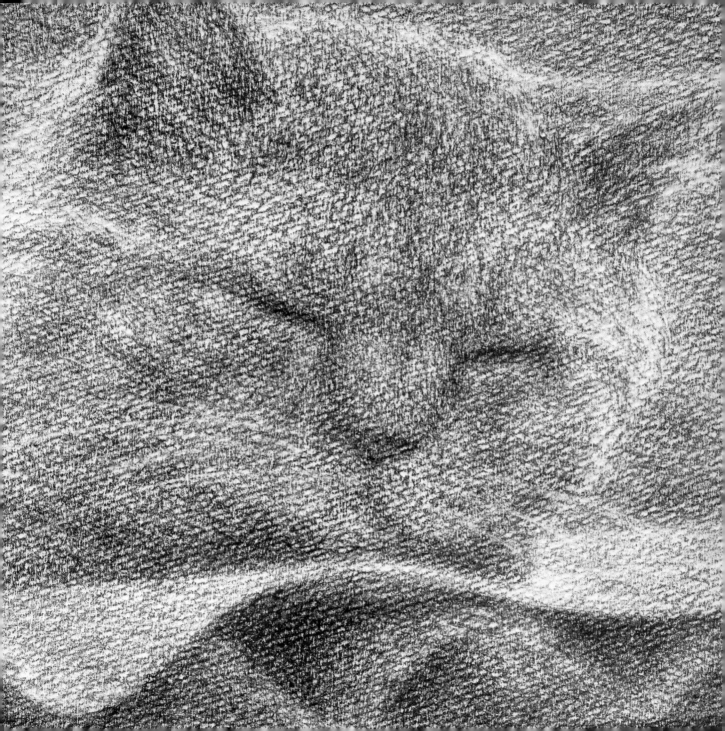

2014년, 집에서 10분 거리의 마을이 폭격을 맞은 듯이 붕괴된 모습을 인터넷에서 처음 보게 되었다.

폭격 소리는 듣지 못했다. 이웃 마을은 사라지는데 무심히 살아간다.

그곳은 지금 사직 롯데캐슬더클래식이 한층 한층 매일매일 올라간다.

대단지 롯데캐슬더클래식 바로 앞 마을도 곧 사직 아시아드쌍용예가가 2018년 생겨날 예정이다.

롯데캐슬이 한 층씩 올라갈 때 이곳은 한 집씩 비워지고 나날이 지워지겠지.

시간이 지나고 생각 없이 여명중학교 옆길을 걸을 나는 폭격 맞은 듯한 모습에 또다시 놀랄 테지.

2016년 5월. 사직 3동. 자전거 바퀴 아래 앉은.

In 2014, at home, I found a photo on the internet that shows a village reduced to rubble.

The village in the photo is 10 minute walk distance from my house.

I have not heard the sound which might be generated while breaking down houses.

My neighboring village is disappearing, but I am living indifferently as usual.

There, these days, apartment called Lotte Castle Classic is being built, a floor higher and higher every day.

And another construction of apartment will start soon.

As times went by, I used to walk around there, passing a middle school nearby,

the desolate scene still comes as shock to me.

May, 2016. Sajik 3dong, Busan. Under a bike wheel.

38

"보상금, 처음에는 보상금이 문제였는지도 몰라요. 너무 터무니없었으니까.

여기가 우리 집이고, 우리가 평생을 가꾸고 생활해온 터전인데 터무니없는 보상금을 제시 하는 게 화가 났어요.

그 돈으로 우리가 갈수 있는 데는 어디일까요? 막말로 누울 자리만 있으면 살 수는 있어요.

그런데 우리는 묻고 싶어요. 우리가 왜 그래야하죠?

내가 생활하고 아끼던 집과 마을에서 왜 우리가 떠나야하죠?

우리는 이곳에, 내가 살던 곳에서 살고 싶을 뿐이에요. 우리는 왜 쫓겨 가야 하나요?"

······ 만덕주민공동체

2016년 5월. 만덕사랑방 근처 적재된 철근 아래에.

"In the first place, compensation mattered. It was so ridiculous.

We have our home here; we have built up our living base at this house.

We were angry with the ridiculous compensation they suggested.

Where can we go with the compensation money to live elsewhere?

Yes, probably, we can live somewhere else, but why do we have to be kick out from where we have lived,

just taking the compensation money they suggest?

I have lived and cared my house, why we have to leave here?

We just want to keep on living here as we have done."

······ Speak out from Manduck Daechoonanmoo Gol community.

May, 2016. Under piles of rebar near Manduck resident community center.

만덕 사랑방에 갔다가 마을에서 만나게 된 고양이. 적의를 띤 눈빛으로 한동안 가만히 서 있었다.
너는 누구고 이곳에 왜 왔는지를 묻는 듯한 눈빛. 계속되는 내안의 질문과 같은 질문.
답을 듣지 않아도 고양이는 이내 긴장을 풀고 부서진 집터 위에서 나를 바라보며 몸을 누인다.
다시 찾아갔을 때 고양이가 누워있던 부서진 집터조차 사라졌다.
부서진 그곳을 지키며 떠나지 않던 고양이들은 어디로 쫓겨 갔을까?

2016년 5월.

A cat I met at Manduck Sarangbang. She stared at me with hostile eyes for a while.
She looked as if she asked me what made you come here, and who you are.
It was the same question as I asked myself.
Why I come here again? I did not answer,
but she was lying down on the ruined house as if she was told an answer from me.
When I came next time, the collapse house was removed. Where the cat has gone now?

May, 2016.

"나는 이곳에서 태어났어요, 이곳에서 결혼도 하고 아이도 낳았어요.
그런데 밤에 길을 잃어 버렸어요. 내가 걷던 길을 알아볼 수 가 없어요.
내가 알아보던 것들이 다 무너져 내렸어요. 감각에 마비가 오는 거 같아요."
"..70년대 이주해서 이 마을엔 고령자들이 많이 살아왔어요. 이제 와서 어디로 갈 수 있겠습니까?
월세를 구한다 해도 어떻게 월세를 감당하겠습니까?
어디에도 살 수 없는 보상금을 받고 나가라니, 누가 그걸 받아들일 수 있겠습니까?"
······ 만덕주민공동체

2016년 5월. 몇 채 남지 않은 만덕의 집들, 옥상의 그늘 아래.

"I was born here, and married and gave birth to a baby here. However, I lost here at night.
I could not figure out where I have to go. The directions I used to know do not exist anymore.
Houses and buildings existed were all gone. I feel like I was paralyzed and lost."
"In this village, there live many old migrants from other provinces in 1970s.
Where they can live after leaving here.
If they rent a house, how these old people can managed to pay monthly rent fee?
How can they accept the compensation and leave here?"
······ Speak out from Manduck Daechoonanmoo Gol community.

May, 2016. Few houses are left in Manduck village. Under the shadows of roofs.

길을 잃은

cats that lost

부산대 앞 래미안 아파트가 들어선다는 자리.
2014년 4월 라일락, 동백꽃, 목련꽃, 벚꽃이 피고
고양이들은 꽃 속에서 옥상 햇볕 아래 옹기종기 앉아
사진 찍던 나와 선배를 구경하던…

In the areas before Busan National University, where Raemian apartments are being built.
2014, April, spring time, lilac, camellias, magnolia, cherry blossoms have already blossomed,
and cats were sitting in huddle around the trees.
They were watching me and my friend taking photos of them in curiosity.

2015년 6월. 부산 황새알 마을.
잔뜩 긴장하다가도 이내 긴장을 풀고
햇볕 쪽을 바라보는 당신의 몸.

June, 2015. Hwangsaeal village, Busan.
Your body was on full alert and soon turned your body to sunshine.

태어난 지 두 달이 안 된 듯한 네가 태어난 곳은 무너지는 마을에 부서진 집.

말라 가는 하루하루를 딛고 서는 래미안. 너에게 줄 수 있는 한 줌도 쥐고 있지 않는.

그리고 가늘게 뜬 눈.

A baby cat seemed to have just born within 2months.
You birthplace is a shattered house in ruined place.
Raemian apartments are building up and up everyday, which are withering every life here.
I have nothing to feed you, baby cat. You just watch me, with feeblish, almost closed eyes.

아이들과 당신을 병들게 하는 세상과
아파하는 모습을 무단 침입하여 바라보는 나에 대한 적의.

This world suffers you and your children and
I am invader of your territory to see you suffering
and you watched me back with hostility in your eyes.
They were watching me and my friend taking photos of them in curiosity.

2015년 5월. 부산 대연 4동.
잘린 나무 그루터기 위.
다시 만나게 되어 반가운 당신.

May, 2015. Daeyondong, Busan.
On a tree stump,
so glad to see you again.

황무지가 된 넓은 터. '크고 강한' 부산 시청이 마주 서 있는 곳.
멀리 서 있는 낯선 이를 바라보며 흙밭을 구르는 '작고 어여쁜' 너의 천진함을.

Across wide vacant lot like wasteland, 'big and great' Busan City Hall stands.
You, little adorable creature, too ingenuous to
greet a stranger like me and roll on dusty ground.

다 무너져 내린 부산 장전 3지구 옆을 지나다 보게 된.
2014년에 빈집 옥상에서 해를 쬐던 고양이었을까? 폐허 위 뒤엉킨 넝마 위에 몸을 누이고.

Passing collapsed Jangeong 3dong, Busan, I saw a cat. Is she the cat that I saw on the roof of vacant house, being bathed in sun? Lying down on ragged cloths among shattered houses.

한 겨울의 부산 명륜 4지구. 가만히 앉아있던 노란 고양이.

Midwinter Myungryoon 4dong, Busan. Yellowish cat sitting still.

'그린 스타트! 녹색은 생활이다!' 녹색 건설을 위해 실천한다는 건설사는 부산 만덕 5지구의
수많은 대추나무, 향나무, 앵두나무들을 모두 잘라버리고 있다.
철거가 시작된 2015년 겨울 1월 추위에 웅크리고 침입자를 경계하고 있는.

'Green Start! Green is your everyday life' Construction companies claim they 'build Green',
they are logging up all trees, jujube tree, prunus tomentosa.
That winter, January 2015, when demolition of houses began.
They are on alert, and crouched their bodies because of harsh coldness.

2015년 1월 부산 만덕 5지구.
늦은 오후 햇살을 등지고
동그랗게 앉아있는 하얀색 신체,
철거가 시작된 겨울.

January, 2015. Manduck 5dong, Busan.
Late afternoon, Round shaped body
under the sunshine.
That winter when demolition began.

2015년 1월. 부산 대연 4동 철거촌.
웅크린 몸.

January, 2015. Daeyon 4dong, Busan.
Fully crouched body.

2015년 1월. 부산 대연 4동 철거촌.
오전 햇볕을 쬐며 파괴된 집들을 가린 베일 앞에.

January, 2015. Daeyon 4dong, Busan.
Cat in front of the veil covering debris of destroyed houses.

2015년 1월. 부산 대연 7지구.
집이 해체되어 무덤이 된 언덕, 검은색 그물천 덮인 곳에 앉아 곳곳에서 삐져나온 철근으로 두 눈이 가리어진.

January, 2015. Daeyoen 7dong, Busan.
Shattered houses now seem to turn to a great tomb, being covered with black cloth.
The cat's eyes are covered with rebar that is seen on the black cloth here and there.

2015년 5월. 부산 못골.
당신의 마을과 당신의 터전이
서서히 부서져가는 것을 목격한 자이자,
폐허에서 구조되지도 못한 당신.
그 폐허 위에 가만히 앉아있는 당신.

May, 2015. Motgol, Busan.
You are the witness how your shelter,
your village have been being destroyed
and you were not rescued from the destruction.
And you still stay on the deserted land.

2015년 5월. 부산 대연동 철거 지구.
당연한 분노와 적의.

May, 2015. Daeyoendong, Busan.
Justifiable anger and hostility.

2015년 6월. 부산 황새알 마을.

은신처에 숨어있는 친구를 지키며 앉은 의젓하고 고운 님.

June, 2015. Hwangsaeal village, Busan.

Gracefully, you are guarding your friends hiding in their sanctuary.

2016년 3월. 부산 명륜 4지구.
싱크홀에 갇힌 듯한, 빠져나오지 못한 목소리. 작고 슬픈 울음.

March, 2016. Myungryoon 4dong, Busan.
As if buried in a sink hall, voice failed to come out. Low and sad weeping.

2016년 3월. 부산 명륜 4지구.
천천히 다가오는 아픈 다리.

March, 2016. Myungryoon 4dong, Busan.
I had walked long, I felt my legs got soured.

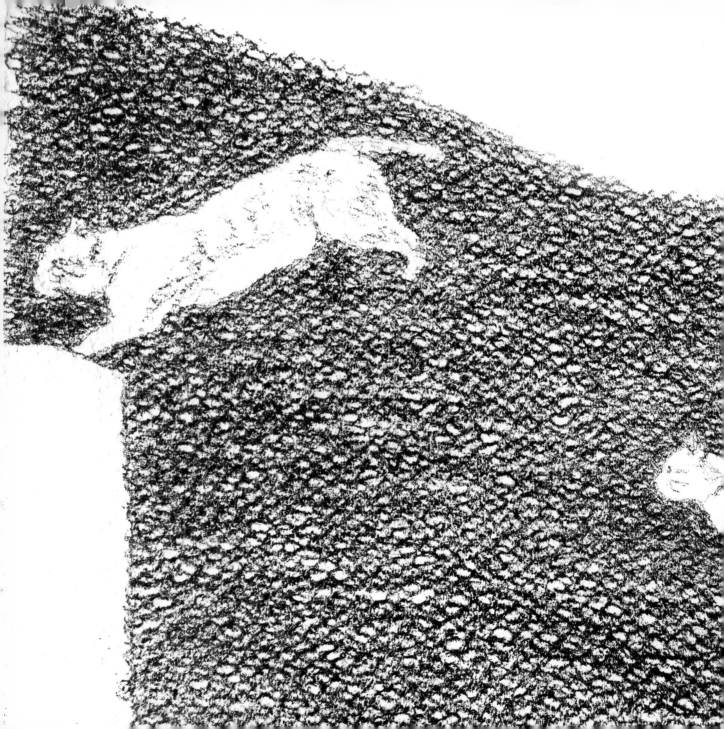

2016년 3월. 부산 온천 2지구.
금정산 아래 소나무가 많은 마을. 사라질 마을. 아마도.
집 담장과 집 사이를 날으는 고양이. 달구어진 차 위에서 잠자는 고양이.
아직은 평화로운 듯 보인다.

A village full of pine trees at the bottom of Geumjeong Mountain.
A cat jumping over a house to other house.
A cat sleeping on a car. At least, so far, peaceful scenery.

2016년 3월. 부산 명륜 4지구. 지구 별, 개기일식.
거대한 왕릉처럼 쌓인 콘크리트 부서진 무덤.
집을 잃고 떠도는 큰 개를 피해 콘크리트 무덤 위에 앉은
고양이 뒤로 보이는 롯데백화점. 백화점 옆 폐허.

Myungryoon 4dong, Busan. Earth, Total Eclipse.
High concrete tomb like King's tomb in the past.
A cat flees to on concrete tomb to avoid big fierce dog. Behind the tomb,
Lotte department store is seen from far. Next to the department, there is wide ruined lot.

2015년 1월. 부산 대연 7지구.
한 집 한 집 부서지는 마을에 바닥에 널브러진
이불, 쓰레기 봉지, 철근 뒤에 숨어서.

January, 2015. Daeyoen 7dong, Busan.
On the ground of crumbled houses of village,
cat hiding behind abandoned
blankets, plastic bags, rebar.

Where have all the cats gone?

writing and drawing / Park Jahuyn
interview / Lee Sookyung
translation / Lee Jeongsil
edit and design / Kim Chuljin
proofreading / Bak Jihyung

ISBN 978-89-90969-95-8 03810

Price / 12,000 Won

고양이들은
어디로 갔을까?

지은 이 / **박자현**
펴낸 날 / 2016년 10월 28일
펴낸 이 / **김철진**
펴낸 곳 / **비온후** www.beonwhobook.com
　　　　　등록 2000년 4월 28일(제2011-000004호)

글 · 그림 / **박자현**
번역 / **이정실**
인터뷰 / **이수경**
디자인 / **김철진**
교정 / **박지형**
제작 진행 / **삼원 D&P**

ISBN 978-89-90969-95-8 03810

책값 / 12,000원